ADVENTURE TIME™

RIGHTEOUS RULES
FOR BEING AWESOME

by Jake Black

PSS!

PRICE STERN SLOAN
An Imprint of Penguin Group (USA) Inc.

PRICE STERN SLOAN
Published by the Penguin Group
Penguin Group (USA) Inc., 375 Hudson Street, New York, New York 10014, USA
Penguin Group (Canada), 90 Eglinton Avenue East, Suite 700,
Toronto, Ontario M4P 2Y3, Canada
(a division of Pearson Penguin Canada Inc.)
Penguin Books Ltd., 80 Strand, London WC2R ORL, England
Penguin Group Ireland, 25 St. Stephen's Green, Dublin 2, Ireland
(a division of Penguin Books Ltd.)
Penguin Group (Australia), 250 Camberwell Road, Camberwell, Victoria 3124, Australia
(a division of Pearson Australia Group Pty. Ltd.)
Penguin Books India Pvt. Ltd., 11 Community Centre, Panchsheel Park,
New Delhi—110 017, India
Penguin Group (NZ), 67 Apollo Drive, Rosedale, Auckland 0632, New Zealand
(a division of Pearson New Zealand Ltd.)
Penguin Books (South Africa) (Pty.) Ltd., 24 Sturdee Avenue,
Rosebank, Johannesburg 2196, South Africa

Penguin Books Ltd., Registered Offices: 80 Strand, London WC2R ORL, England

Published in 2012 by Price Stern Sloan, a division of Penguin Young Readers Group, 345 Hudson Street, New York,
New York 10014. *PSS!* is a registered trademark of Penguin Group (USA) Inc. Printed in the U.S.A.

ISBN 978-0-8431-7223-2   10 9 8 7 6 5 4 3 2

ALWAYS LEARNING   PEARSON

How to Use This Book

Welcome to the Land of Ooo. I know you always wanted to visit here, but just never had the time, or the chance, or the guts. A lot of crazy stuff happens here, and it's always up to my friend Finn and me to save the day. We've fought evil ice kings, vampires, and other nutso baddies. Every day is an adventure. And I know you want to be just like us. That's why Finn and I put together this book for you. We know we're your heroes and you want to be just like us. Ain't that right, Finn?

That's right, Jake. No one should ever come to the Land of Ooo without having adventurer training. Really no one should try to live their life anywhere without learning how to be as awesome, tough, and smart as I am! And that's what we want to do—teach you how to live your life like Jake and I live ours. You may not live in a magical land of adventure, but you do have your own adventures to go on every day. So, with this book in your hands, you'll learn all the secrets of having an adventurer's life!

So, you're probably wondering what this book is going to teach you. Well, it's everything from how to be brave and fight vampires to how to score points with the ladies. And it's all because we know how to do it!

Well, I know how to do it. Don't listen to Finn. He doesn't know nothing. If you ever wanted to know what it was like to be us—it's pretty awesome, by the way—this is your chance.

Here's how you should use this book:
* To learn the right ways of righteousness
* To make your life as awesome as it can be
* To make you smarter and wiser than anyone else you know

And here's how not to use this book:
* As a weapon to battle enemy warriors
* As a snack when you're hungry
* As a cushion for your hardest chair

FRIENDSHIP

The first thing you need to learn about if you're going to have adventures like ours is friendship. What is a friend? Is it someone with whom you can share your deepest secrets? A confidant who is your moral compass? Your . . .

. . . sidekick, like Jake is for me. It doesn't have to be all that deep mushy stuff Jake was talking about.

Sidekick? Dude, you'd be nothing without me. I might have taught you everything you know, but I didn't teach you everything I know. If anyone's a sidekick, it's you, buddy.

Whatever. I guess we're best friends, not sidekicks. Remember that time you tried to make me and Lady Rainicorn best friends, too? That didn't go too well.

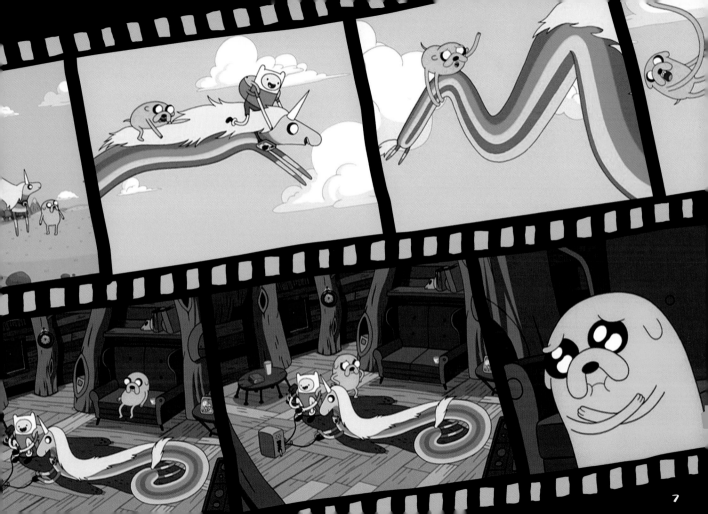

I just wanted my two best friends to be friends so I could hang out with both of you more. How was I supposed to know you guys would become better friends than I was with you? I hated that!

So you went and found Tiffany to make us jealous? That's not a good way to keep your friends! Besides, Lady Rainicorn and I were only jealous for a second. You can have more than one friend, you know.

Yeah, I know. I learned that from that one time when Lady Rainicorn and you . . . oh, wait, I already told that story. You know what else is awesome about friendship? That you can have friends that you wouldn't expect, like a Snow Golem and Fire Wolves.

Like that one time when a Snow Golem found a lost Ice Wolf Cub and helped him get home. The Fire Wolf accidentally melted the Snow Golem, but that didn't matter. Friends help out when times are tough.

12

13

No, I wasn't! Shut up!

Yeah, you were. We fought Ricardio and saved Princess Bubblegum because that's just what friends do. Even if you're in love with her, Finn, you're still her friend.

Having friends is great. Being a friend is better. You know what's the weird thing about being a friend? It gets you more friends. Also, you can have adventures with them.

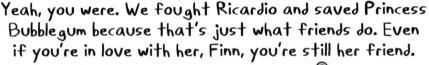

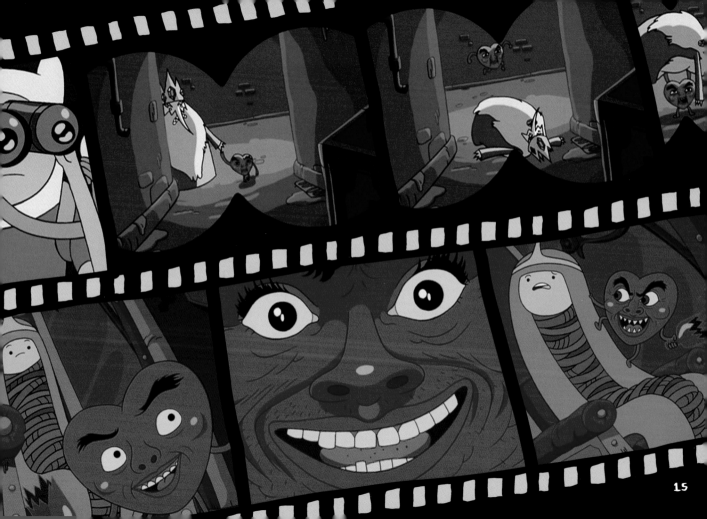

WORK

Everything takes work. It's sad, but true. If you want to buy something, you go to work to earn the money you need for it. If you want to get good at something, you work at it. Everything takes work. Even adventuring.

There are a lot of ways to work. Millions of them, probably. You can work in a store, clean up the house, do your homework for school, babysit the babies . . . Sometimes it can be for money, but mostly it's just because work needs to get done. It can be boring. It can be fun. It's all about attitude, baby.

I hate work.

And that, ladies and gentlemen, is a bad attitude. Just like getting everyone else to do work for you. But this is a bad, bad, bad idea. Finn and I met these businessmen, and they loved to work. They loved it so much that they started doing everything for us.

Yeah, I loved that!

But we got crazy lazy and didn't even get off the couch to save Princess Bubblegum when she needed help! We didn't work and failed as heroes.

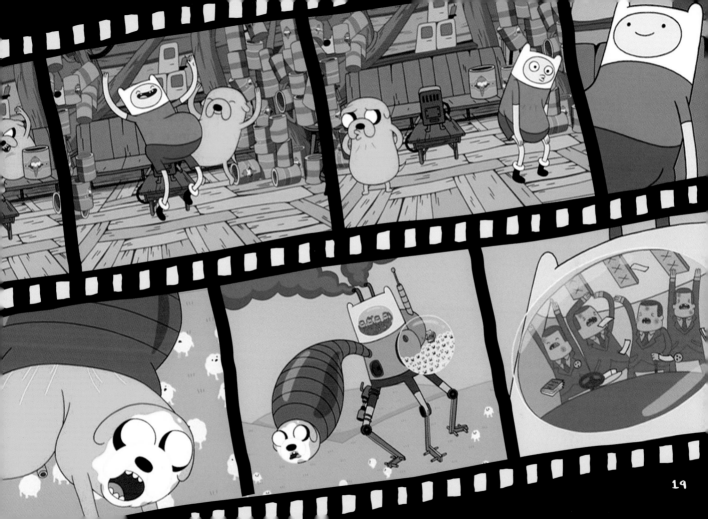

Sometimes you have to work with other people. This can be awesome or super not awesome. You'll have different ideas about how to do stuff and fight. You gotta learn to compromise.

Yeah, compromise. Jake and I made a movie one time, and it was a disaster 'cause we wanted to do it differently. If we'd compromised, it woulda been better.

The next time someone tells you "work stinks," ignore 'em. It might be boring, or hard, or stinky, but it's an important part of life.

Lazy can be fun, though.

23

RECREATION

Not everything is about work. It's important to have fun, too. Have some adventures. It doesn't matter to me what the adventure is, just having one every day. I always feel better about everything in life after I've been on an adventure!

People call it recreation. What is "recreation"? It is the way by which a person re-creates himself. He becomes a new person after having worked his metaphorical "old" person to death. We all must recreate to re-create ourselves.

Dude. Jake. What are you even talking about? What's with all the deep stuff? It's boring. And weird. Recreation is just fun. A lot of fun. That's all there is to it. Have fun. And you feel better! Seriously. Everybody, forget what Jake was saying. Just have fun!

One of the funnest things we've ever done was when we went in this epic maze! It had all these puzzles, and knights, and crazy stuff. So fun! Plus it led to an adventure. If I could go back to that maze and do it again, I totally would!

That maze was fun, I guess. I had to use my stretching powers to their absolute limit, though. That was a lot of work! Not fun for me.

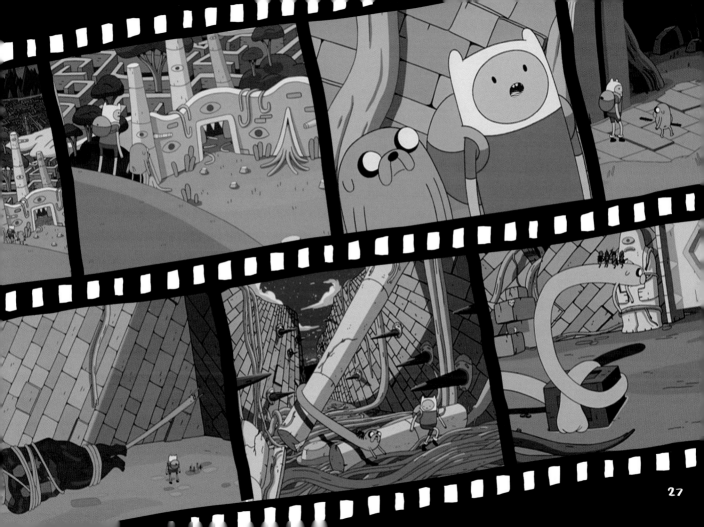

I bet there's people who don't love adventures as much as you do, Finn. I like cooking food more than adventures. Especially the Everything Burrito. Now that's fun!

Yeah, but look at how well that turned out! The creepy, crazy Cuties came and poisoned it. You didn't even get to eat it. You had to bury it in the ground.

I ate it . . . later . . .

Dude! Sick!

28

 Sometimes the most fun is not even doing anything. Then no one will make you have an adventure you don't want.

 Unless a witch steals your powers and that's why you're lazy. Then you have to go on an adventure to get them back.

 All I'm sayin' is that the end result of all of these adventures is that they were fun and made us excited for more fun times. You can call it whatever you want, but I still think it's "re-creating" yourself.

 And I still think all that deep stuff is completely boring. Just have fun. Fun. Fun. Fun. Fun. That's all that matters. Have fun. Your kind of fun. Who cares if other people don't like it? You do, and it makes you feel better. So, go for it!

MAGIC

Magic is the greatest thing in the history of the universe. There. I said it. Magical powers can help you do anything you want whenever you want. But don't use it for evil. If you do, we'll have to stop you and save the world!

I like magic.

The first thing to remember is never use magic wrong because someone could get hurt—or changed into a streetlight or something. The second most important thing to remember about magic is that practice makes perfect. The third thing about magic is that it can't be explained very easily, or at all.

I really like magic.

I've been to wizard school and learned with the other wizard students how to do magic. I had to promise to use my magic for good and take the "Oath of Responsibility," which kinda took the fun out of having magic powers. But at least I got to save the town from a meteor.

Like you did it by yourself. All the other wizards helped you. They were the real heroes.

If I had magic powers right now, you'd so be turned into a toad.

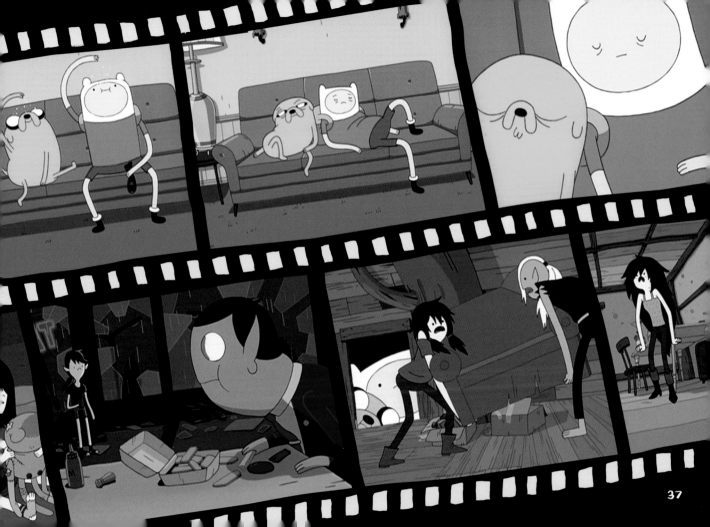

Remember that one time when you got turned into a foot by that hobo? I warned you against giving him food, but did you listen to me? Nope. And magic got used against you. I mean, you were a foot!

Maybe, but you said you always wanted to be a foot and that you were jealous that magic turned me into one.

Looking back it's obvious that magic never turns out well. Memories get erased. People get turned into feet. It's never good. Maybe you should just avoid magic unless you meet a wizard who will give you the power to be perfect at it right away. And I cannot stress this enough. Use it only for good!

I still really like magic.

ROMANCE

Having a girlfriend has been one of the best things that ever happened to me. Lots of people ask me, "Jake, how do you do it? How do get an awesome girlfriend like yours?" Well, it's not easy for most people, but if you're extra smooth with the ladies like I am, it comes completely naturally. Let's give you some advice.

I wish I was smooth with the ladies like you, Jake. Because then I'd get to be with the Princess . . . the Princess . . .

The first thing you gotta do when looking for a lady friend is make sure you're nice and clean. The ladies don't like a dude covered in filth. Or that smells bad.

I don't get it.

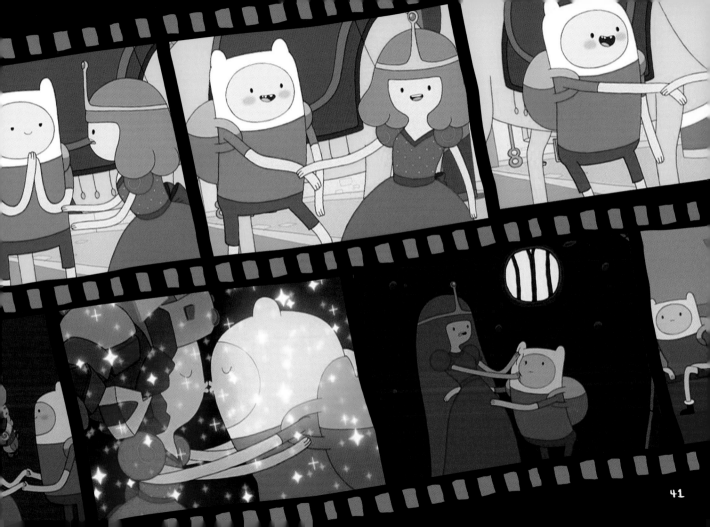

42

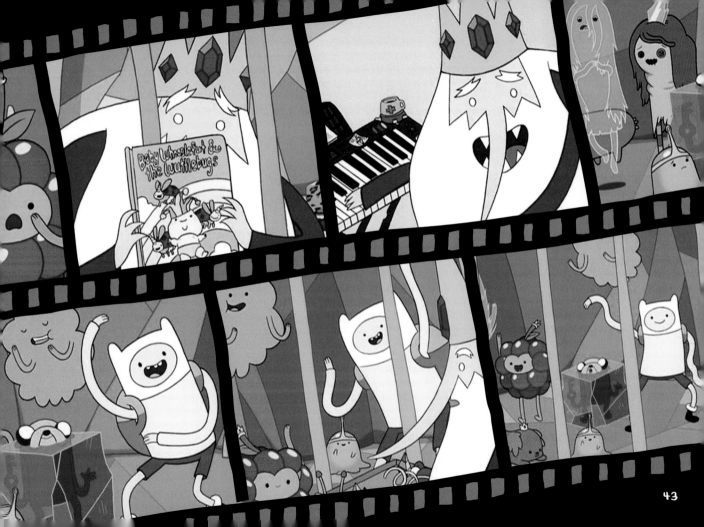

Exactly. Girls like excitement, though. Like I've always said, if you want to get Princess Bubblegum to dig you, you gotta show her an exciting time.

That never works! I tried that one time. It completely freaked her out. I just wanted to go to the movies with her and not make it some big freaking deal thing. But when I tried to make it exciting, it made it a big freaking deal thing!

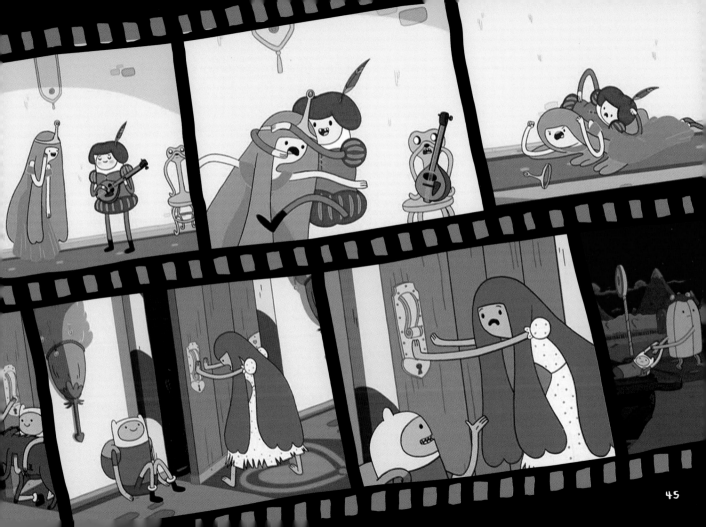

45

Oh yeah. The ladies like a guy who keeps it real. Ice King tried to get some TLC by shaving his beard and calling himself "Nice King." It didn't work because he was trying too hard to be something he's not.

See, that's what I was trying to say from the beginning! You don't have to make yourself all exciting or whatever. Just be yourself!

That's pretty good. But still be cool. Don't be desperate. Don't kidnap. Don't be something you're not. Be nice, but not too nice. Be bold, but not too bold. And shower sometimes.

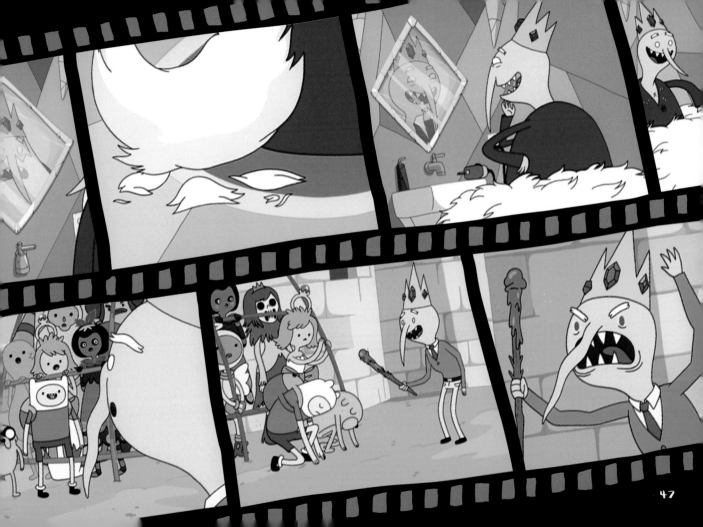

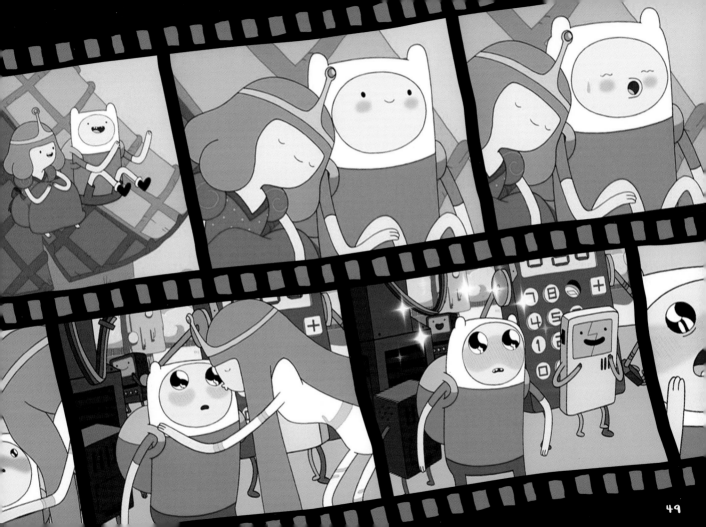

49

OVERCOMING FEAR

I guess it's important to fight back against your fears. I wouldn't know. I'm not scared of anything. At all. I'll show you how to be brave!

Yes, you are. But it's all good, Finn. You have to be scared of something to overcome fear. And you have to overcome fear to be a righteous hero.

But I'm not scared of anything!

Yeah, you are.

Oh yeah? What?

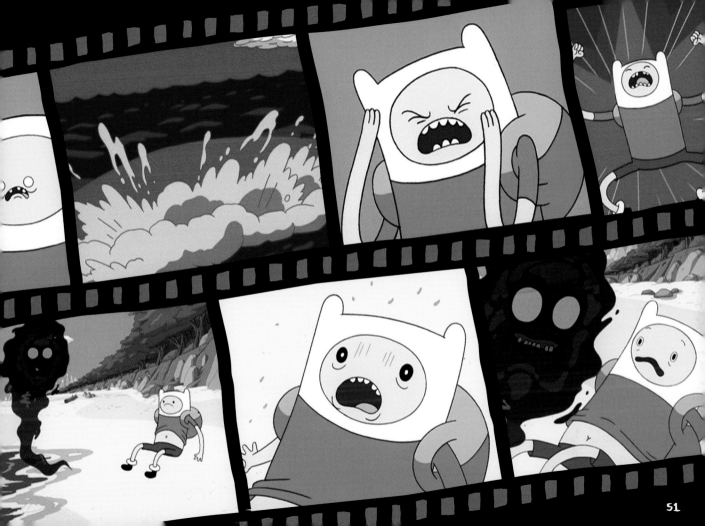

So, not scared of anything.

What about at my birthday when that freaky ghost started killing all the other guests? And you saw that monster. You were wiggin' out pretty good that time.

Not really. I was in on the joke. You set it up with Lady Rainicorn, and I found out about it and knew everything that was happening. I was just pretending to be scared so you'd have a good birthday.

Nope. You were scared for real. You didn't know about my plans until I told you straight up.

54

Whatever. Besides, you're still scared of vampires. Even after Marceline made us think we were vampires and we almost got eaten by her friends.

Um, hello. We *were* almost eaten! That's scary. Vampires. You can't trust them to not eat you. Of course I'm scared of them. A little fear's a good thing. Helps you make smart choices, sometimes. Like not getting eaten by vampires, ghosts, and monsters. Besides, being scared of vampires is way better than being scared of the ocean.

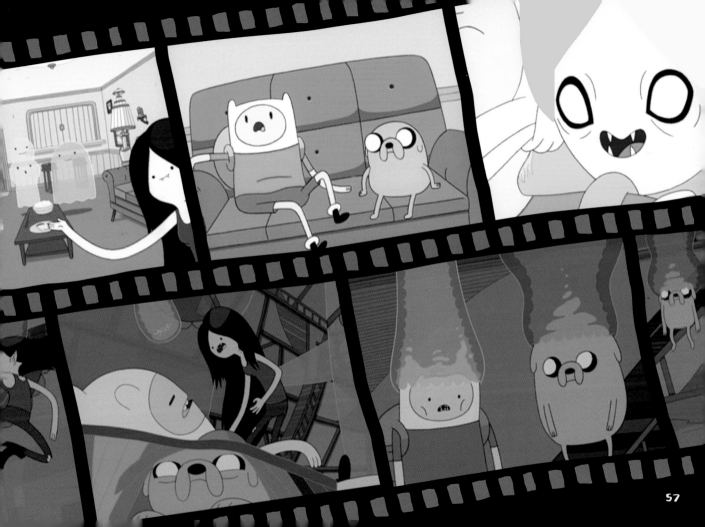

PHYSICAL FITNESS

It's way important for an adventurer to be healthy and strong. I exercise every single day and build up strong muscles so I can go into battle. I'm sure I'm the strongest person in the whole world.

Yeah, that's all good. But you're never as strong or healthy as I am. I'm the greatest athlete of our generation.

I am. You're just a dog with stretch arms.

What? How dare you, sir!

58

60

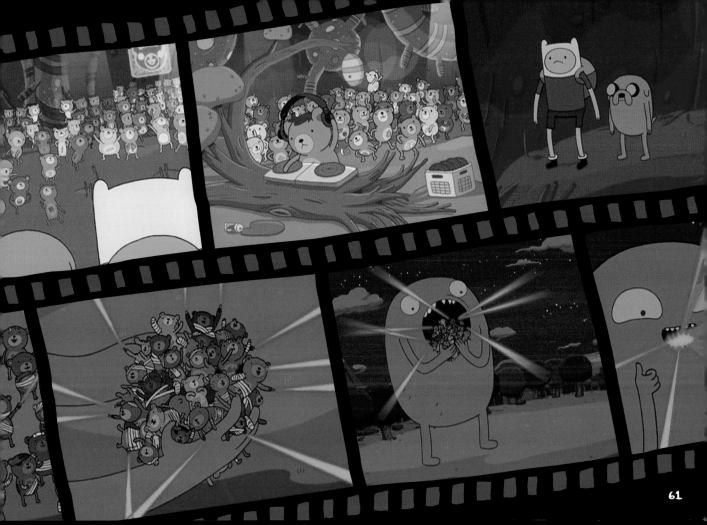

Sometimes you get sick, though. And all the medicine and sleeping and drinking flat lemon-lime soda in the world won't make you feel better. There's only one cure for times like that. A good friend telling you the greatest adventure story ever told.

Hey! I did that for you once!

Duh.

The story I told you only helped because it was so good. And it was only so good because it was true. If you're trying to help a sick friend feel better, you'd better have an awesome adventure to tell them about!

62

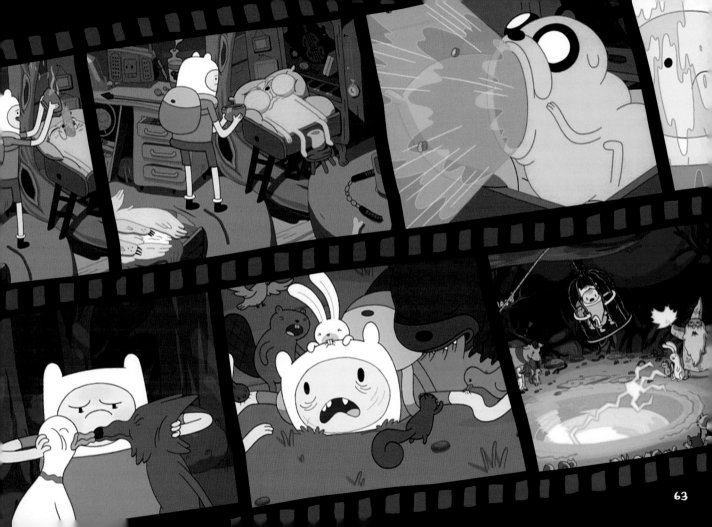

There are no shortcuts to becoming an amazing adventurer. You just have to do the right things all the time!

We've tried shortcuts sometimes, like getting amazing armor that makes you invulnerable, but it was a failure in the big picture. After the armor didn't make me as strong as I thought, I realized I just needed more exercise and better food.

If you eat right, then you'll have enough energy to go outside, run around, and battle monsters. You'll become a hero faster than you can say "you'll become a hero."

Food is yummy. Good food is yummy. Exercise is fun. All of it has made me the strong hero I am today!

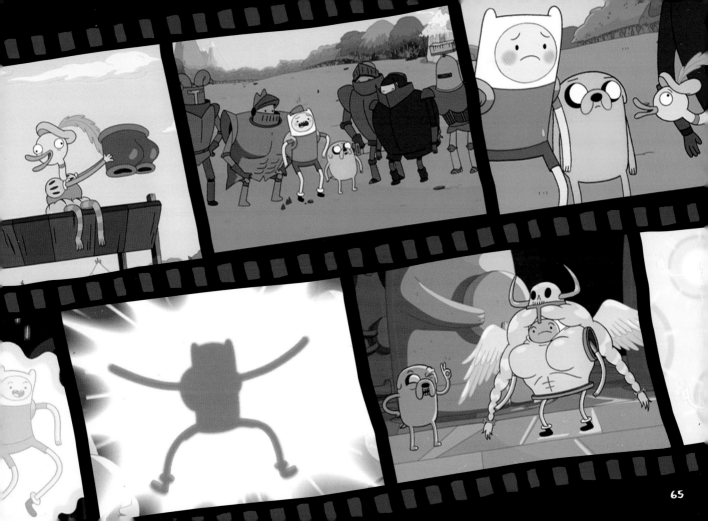

SMARTS

Want to be super good at being an adventurer? You gotta know stuff about stuff. Take me, for instance. I know everything about everything. That's why I'm writing this book for you. To share my vast amounts of knowledge with the universe. You better be paying attention to what I'm telling you or else you won't learn anything. And then you won't know everything about everything!

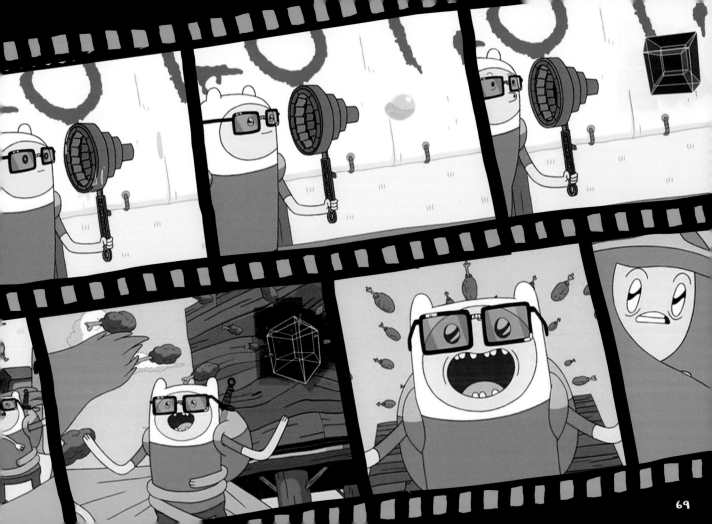

Sometimes there's lots of stuff to distract you from your homework and other stuff that makes you smarter. Stuff like watching TV, playing video games, or anything else that is more fun than homework. It all makes it harder to get smarter. I almost didn't rescue Finn once since I was totally distracted by other fun stuff. Part of getting smarter is ignoring distractions.

Yeah, you got it together, though, and saved me. You gave up your distractions.

Yeah, I'm the man. Anyway, you gotta be smart. You gotta learn how to think. Once you figure out how to think on your own, you can figure out better strategies against enemies. You can build powerful fortresses. You use your imagination to go anywhere anytime.

FAMILY

At the end of a long day of adventuring, it's great to go home and unwind with your family. Finn and I love going home and hanging out with our roommate, BMO. We're like a big, happy family when we get together.

I love you guys!

Lame.

If you didn't have us, what would you do? You'd be bored and lonely and probably get into so much trouble and wouldn't have anyone around you to save you.

Still lame.

I still like you, Finn.

Epically lame.

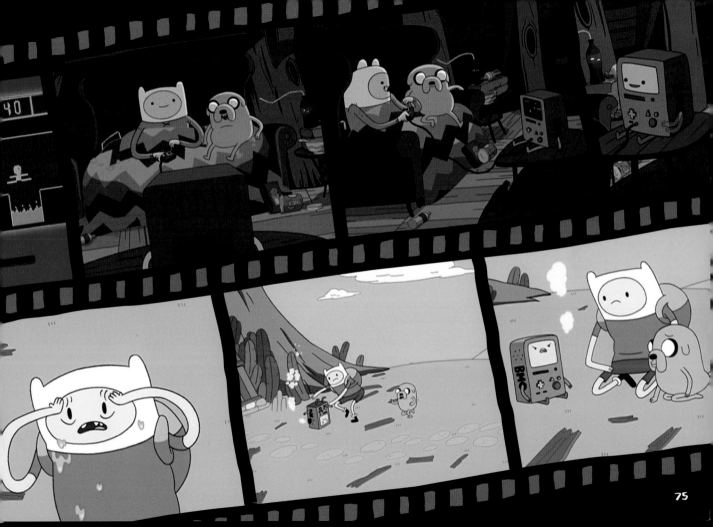

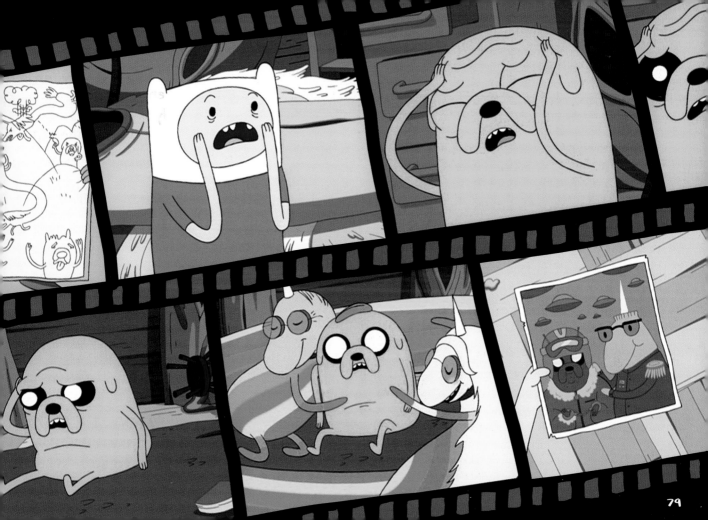

CONCLUSION

So, there you have it. Everything you need to know about how to become a great hero like Finn and me. You gotta have some friends to fight for the right by your side. Everything worth having or worth doing takes a lot of work. But don't only work all the time. Make sure you get in some recreation. Magic can help you in your adventures, but sometimes it makes things worse. To be a true hero, you have to overcome your fears. You can't be a hero if your health is bad, so eat right and exercise. Make sure you study and build up a strong mind, too.

And finally, enjoy your family because they all love and support you.

Fine, I guess it's not really lame. I'm glad I have Jake, BMO, and everybody to have amazing adventurers with.